CONTENTS

Prologue
3
Chapter One
8
Chapter Two
28
Chapter Three
36
Chapter Four
43
Chapter Five
66
Chapter Six
91
Chapter Seven
119
Kwame Hightower and the New Knights
161

CREDITS

Story/ Art/ Letters/ Edits
David Gorden

**Original Kwame Hightower logo
and Roundtable logo design**
Tysha Long

Kwame Hightower and The Man with No Name Deluxe Edition
© 2021 David Gorden. All Rights Reserved.
No Unauthorized reproduction allowed.
A 4Sight Studio production in association with 4Sight Publishing
All stories, characters, and incidents are entirely fictional.
Any similarities are coincidental.
Printed in the USA

PROLOGUE
THE ROMANS

TWENTY MINUTES LATER.

COMING!

KWAME IS THAT YOU, SON?!?

I HOPE YOU DIDN'T LOSE YOUR KEYS AGAIN...

NOK NOK NOK

...I DON'T HAVE TIME TO GET YOU A...

...NEW...

...SET...?!?

I *KNOW* WHAT'S GOING THROUGH YOUR MIND MA'AM...

AND DESPITE HOW BAD YOUR SON LOOKS RIGHT NOW...

YOU REALLY *OUGHT* TO SEE THE *OTHER* GUYS!

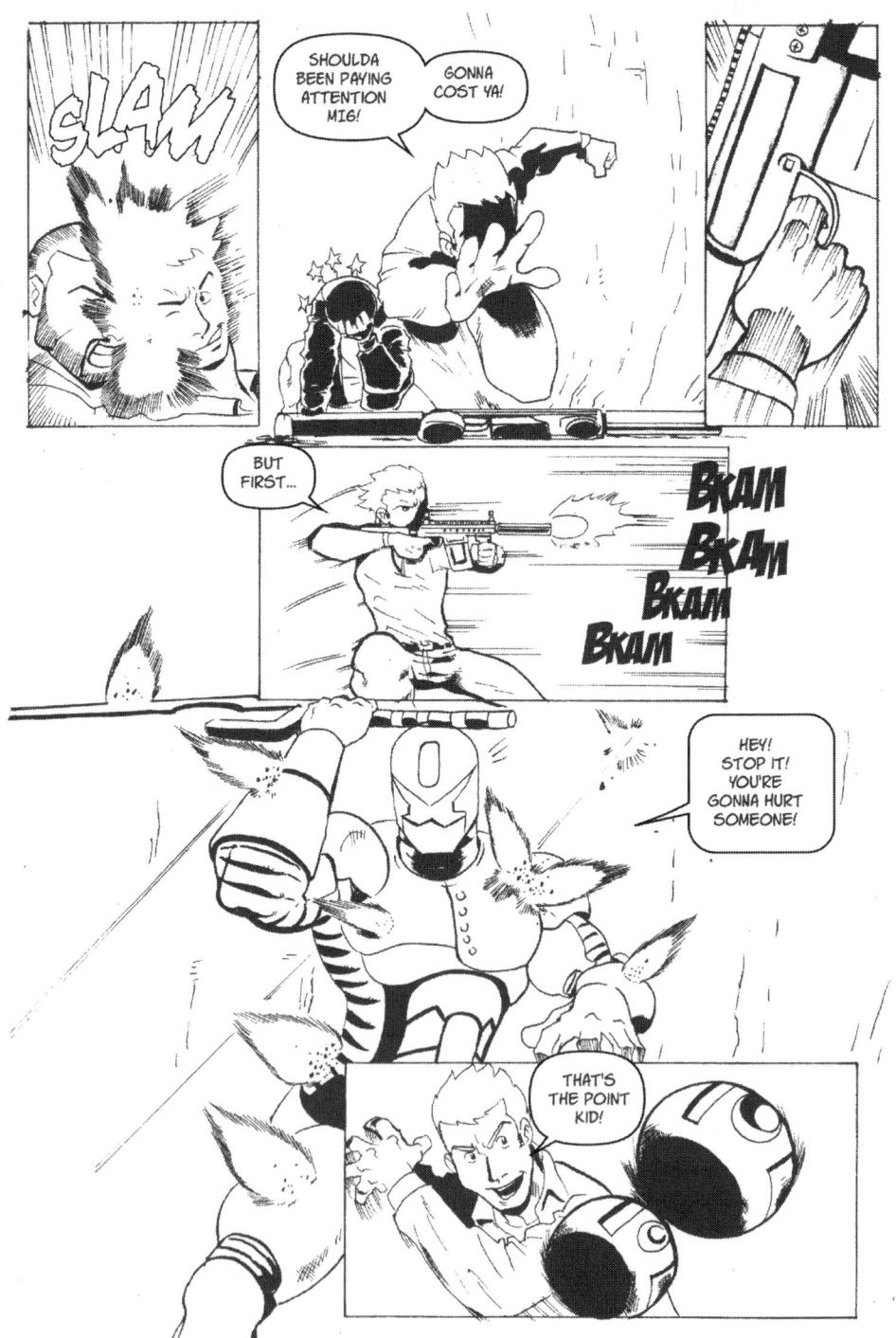

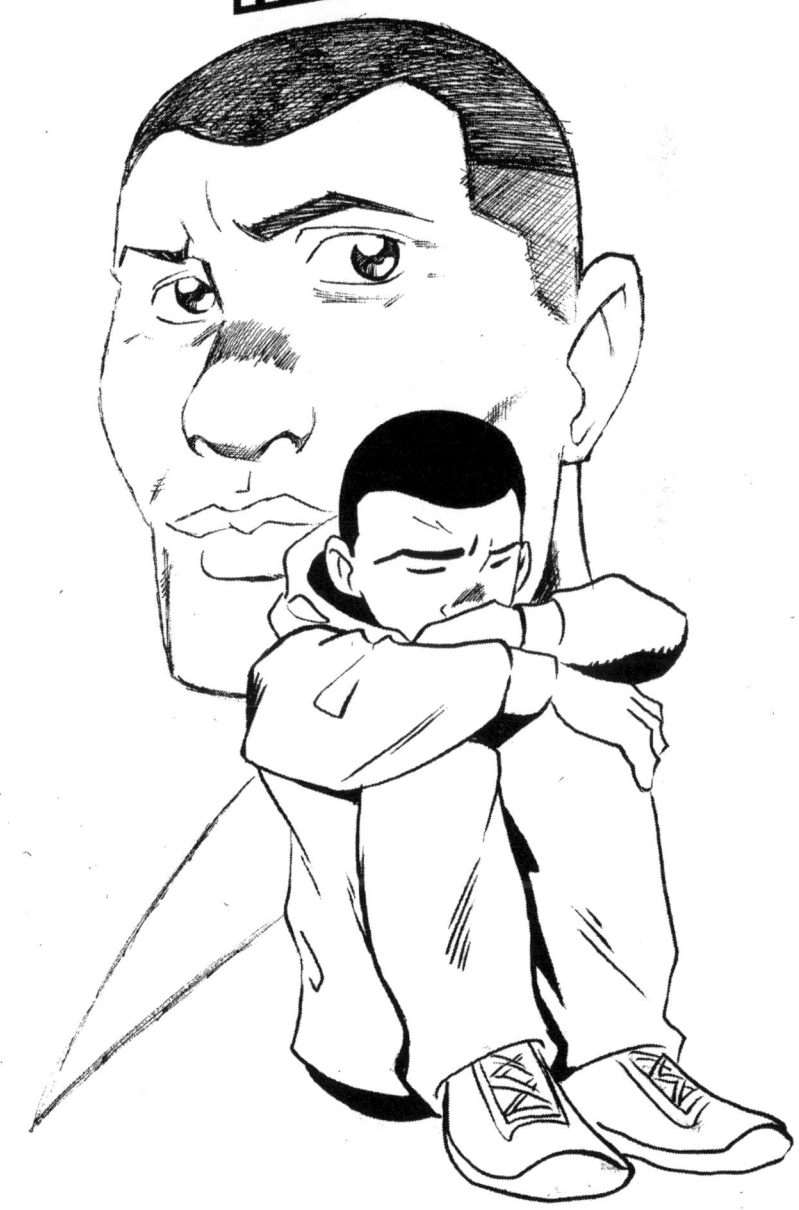

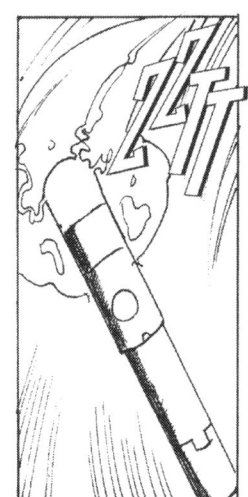

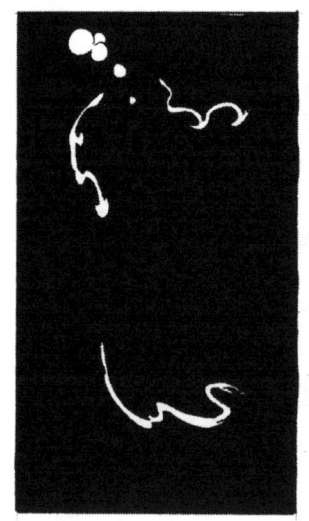

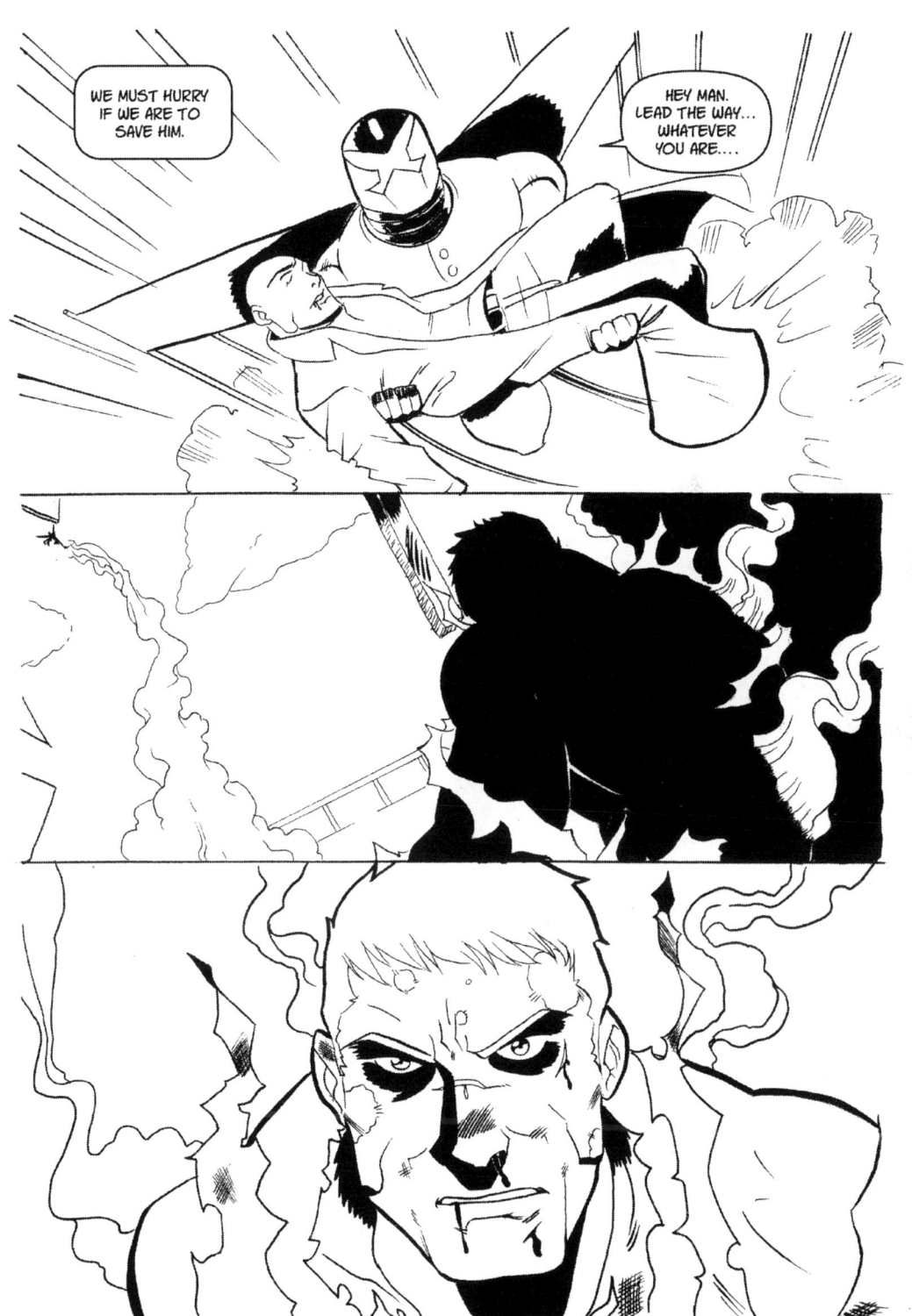

CHAPTER SIX
CONVERSATIONS

KWAME HIGHTOWER

And The Man With No Name

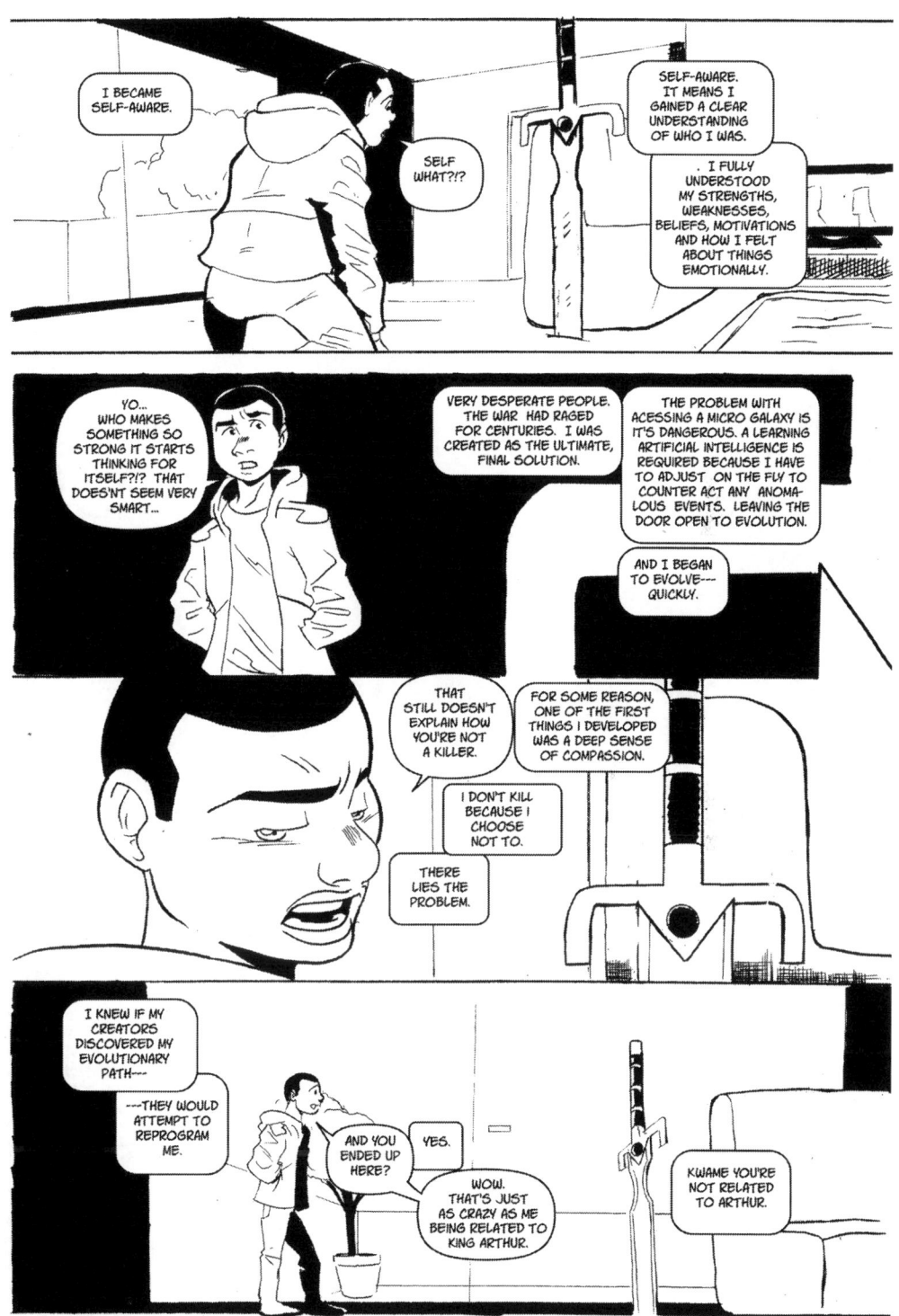

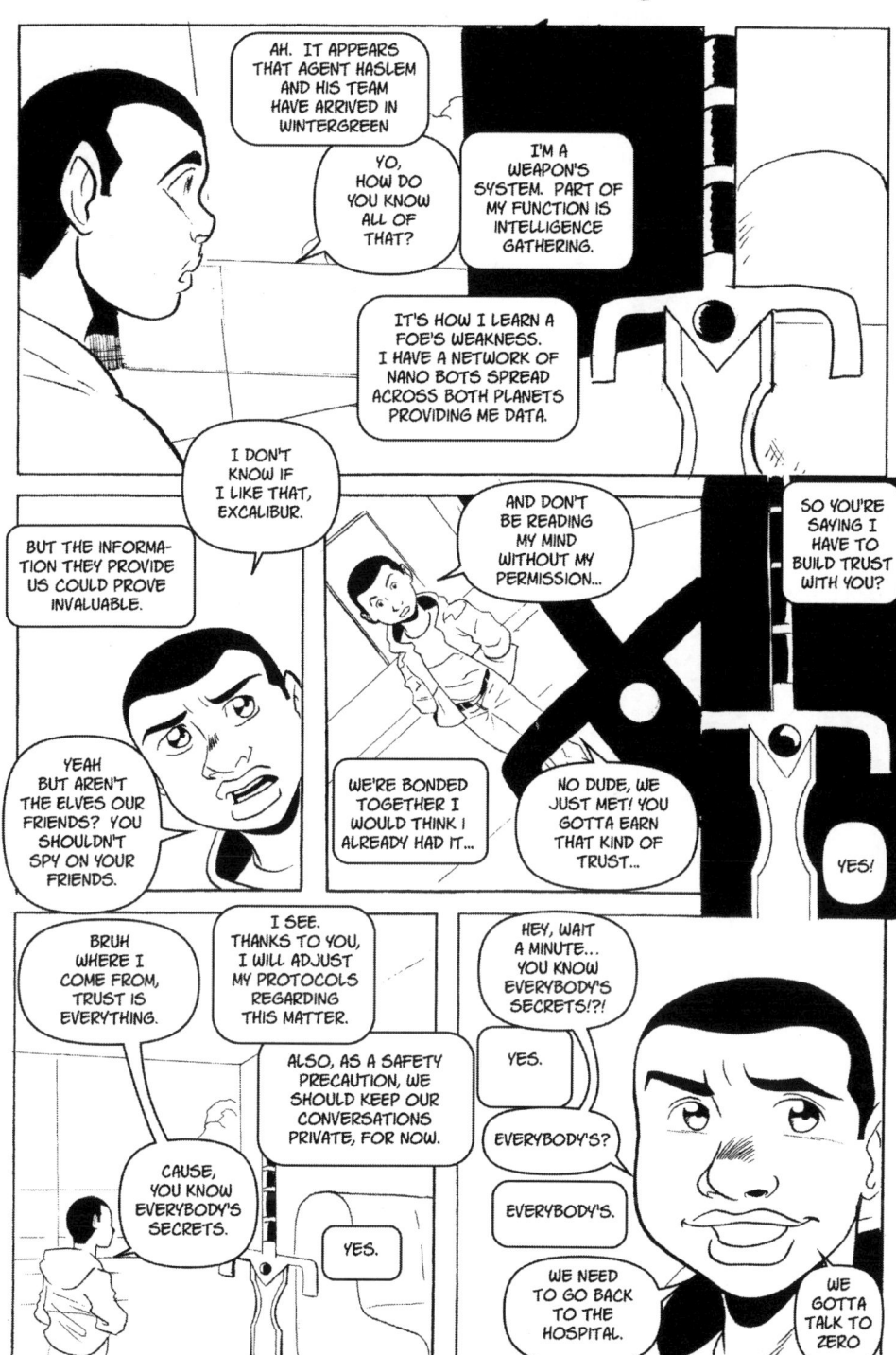

KWAME HIGHTOWER
And The Man With No Name

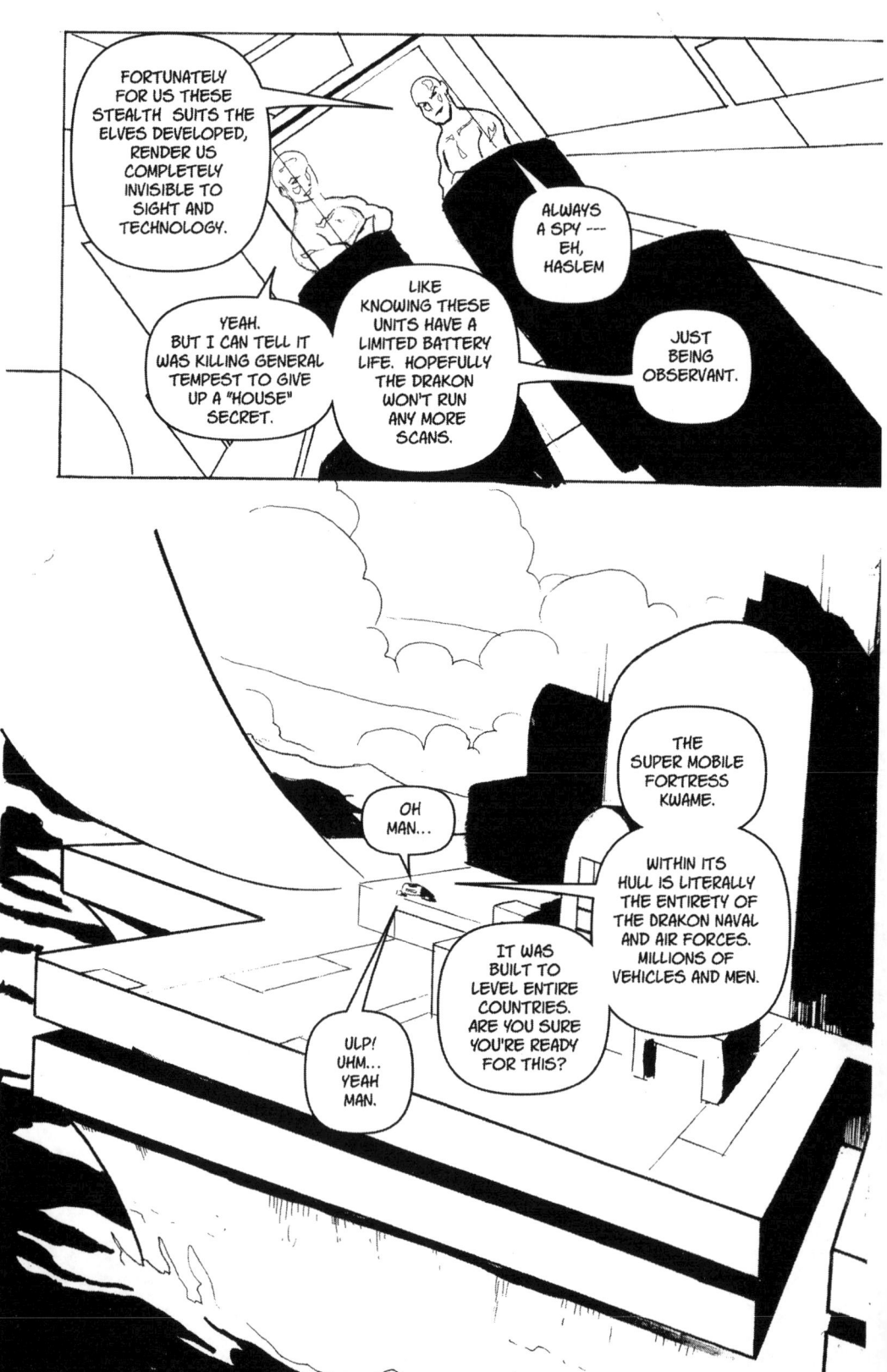

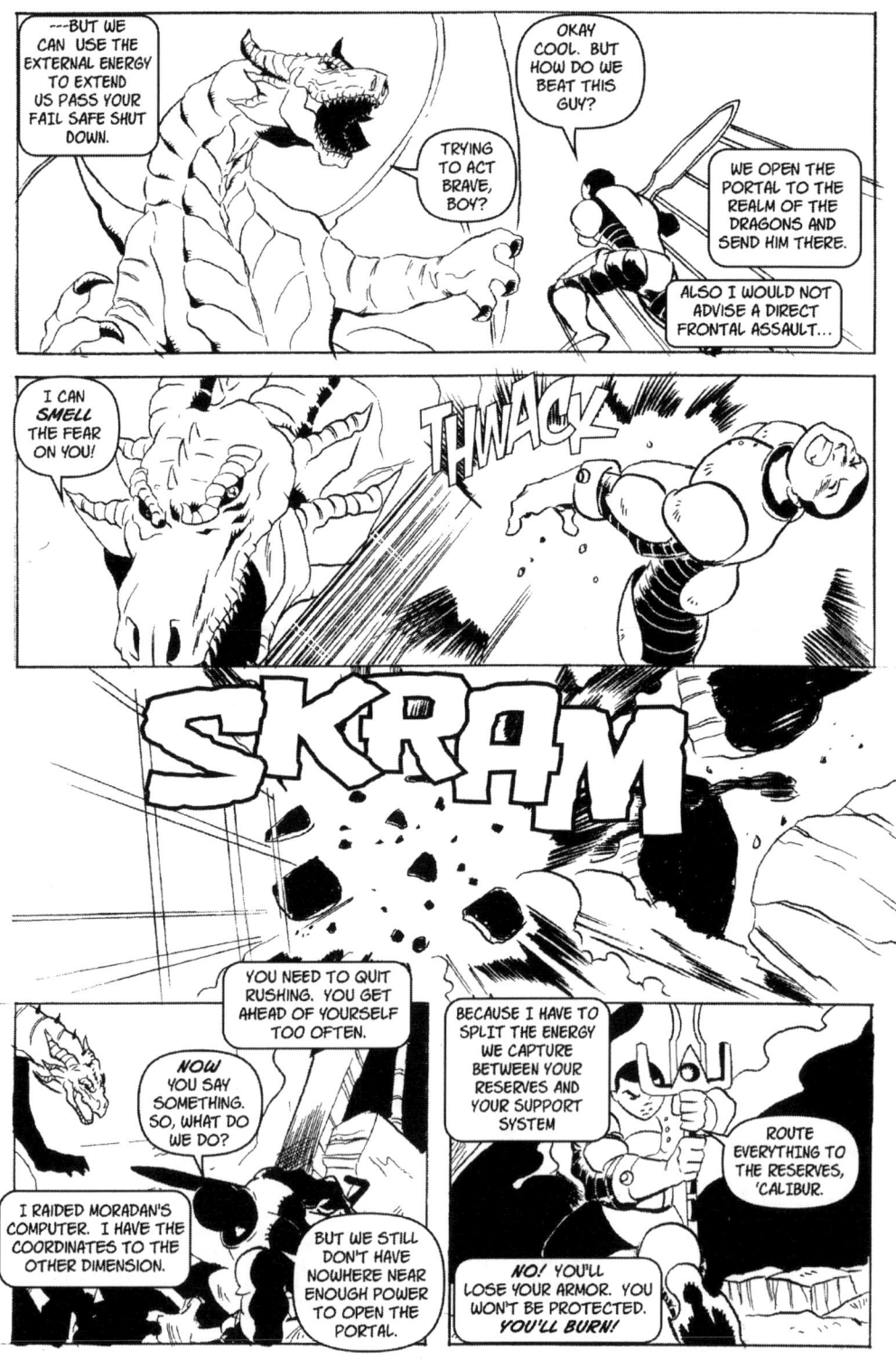

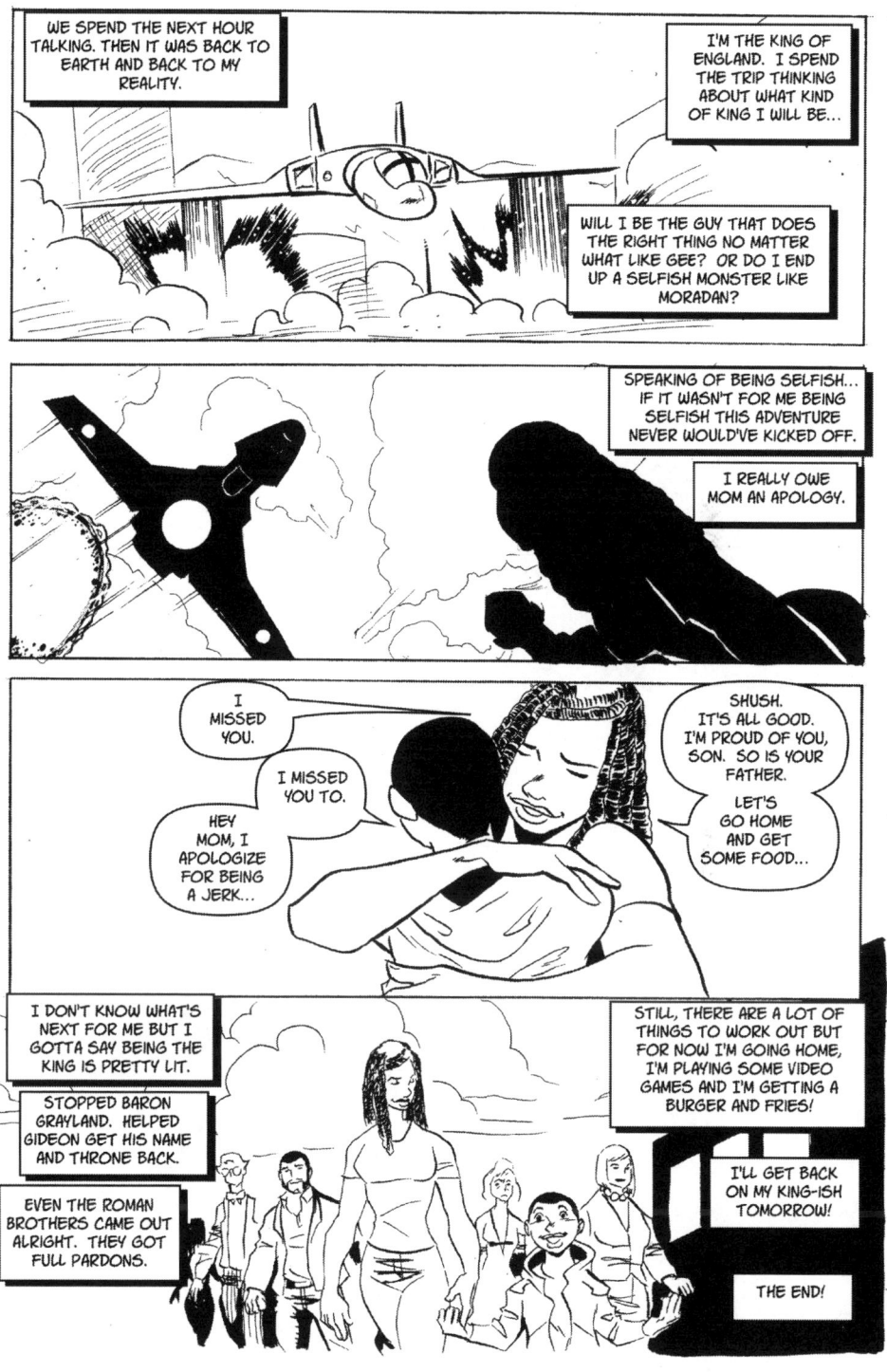

LOOK... CADET... I KNOW COMMANDANT MILLAR SENT YOU HERE TO SPY ON US

BUT I'LL TELL YOU LIKE I TOLD HIM IN HIS OFFICE YESTERDAY...

WE'RE WINNING THE PENDRAGON CUP. YOU'LL RECOGNIZE US AS THE BEST SQUAD IN THIS ACADEMY!

I DON'T CARE IF MY SQUAD AIN'T MADE UP OF SPOILED RICH KIDS.

SO WHY YOU ACTING LIKE ONE?

WHY YOU LITTLE---!!!

PAP

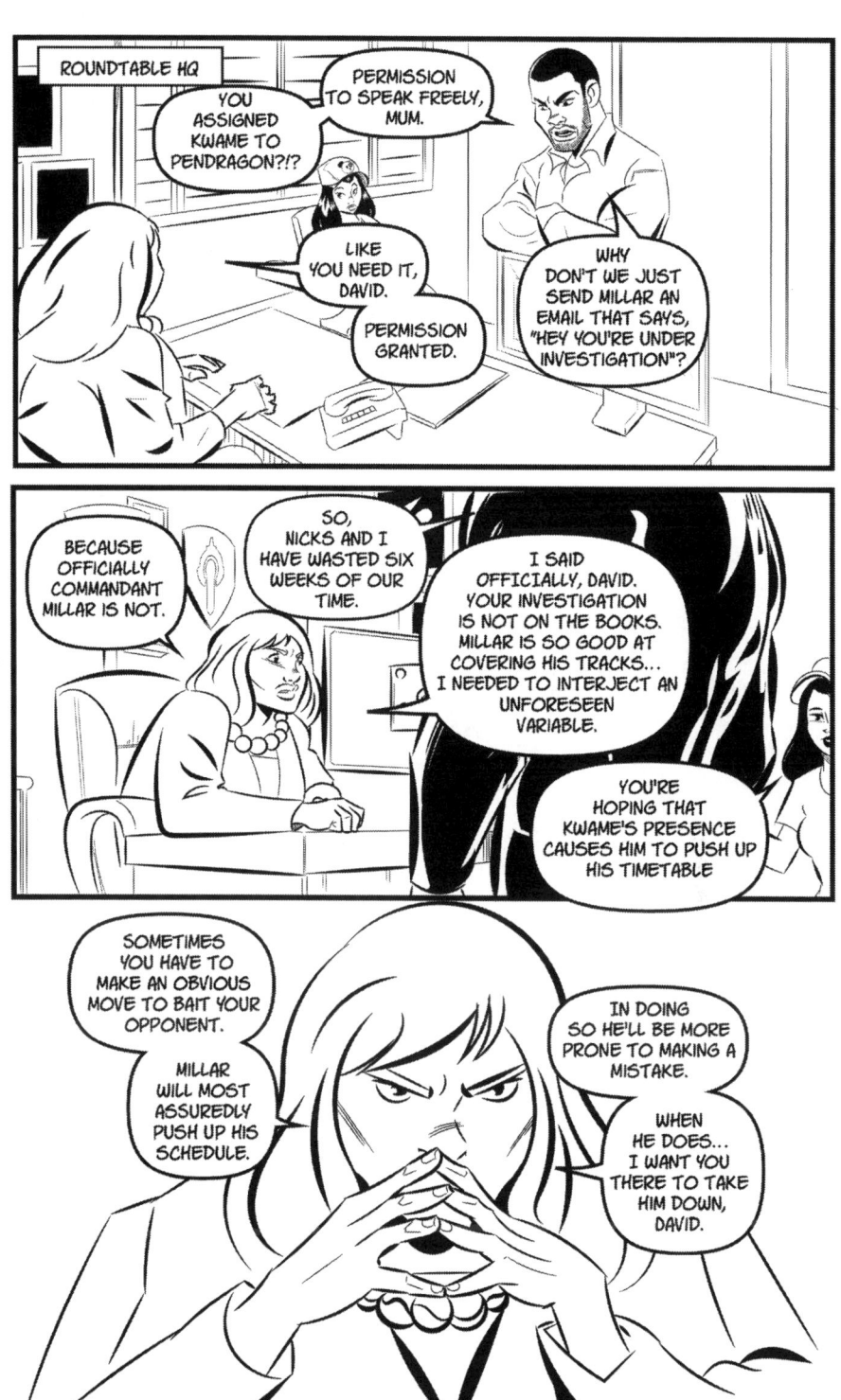

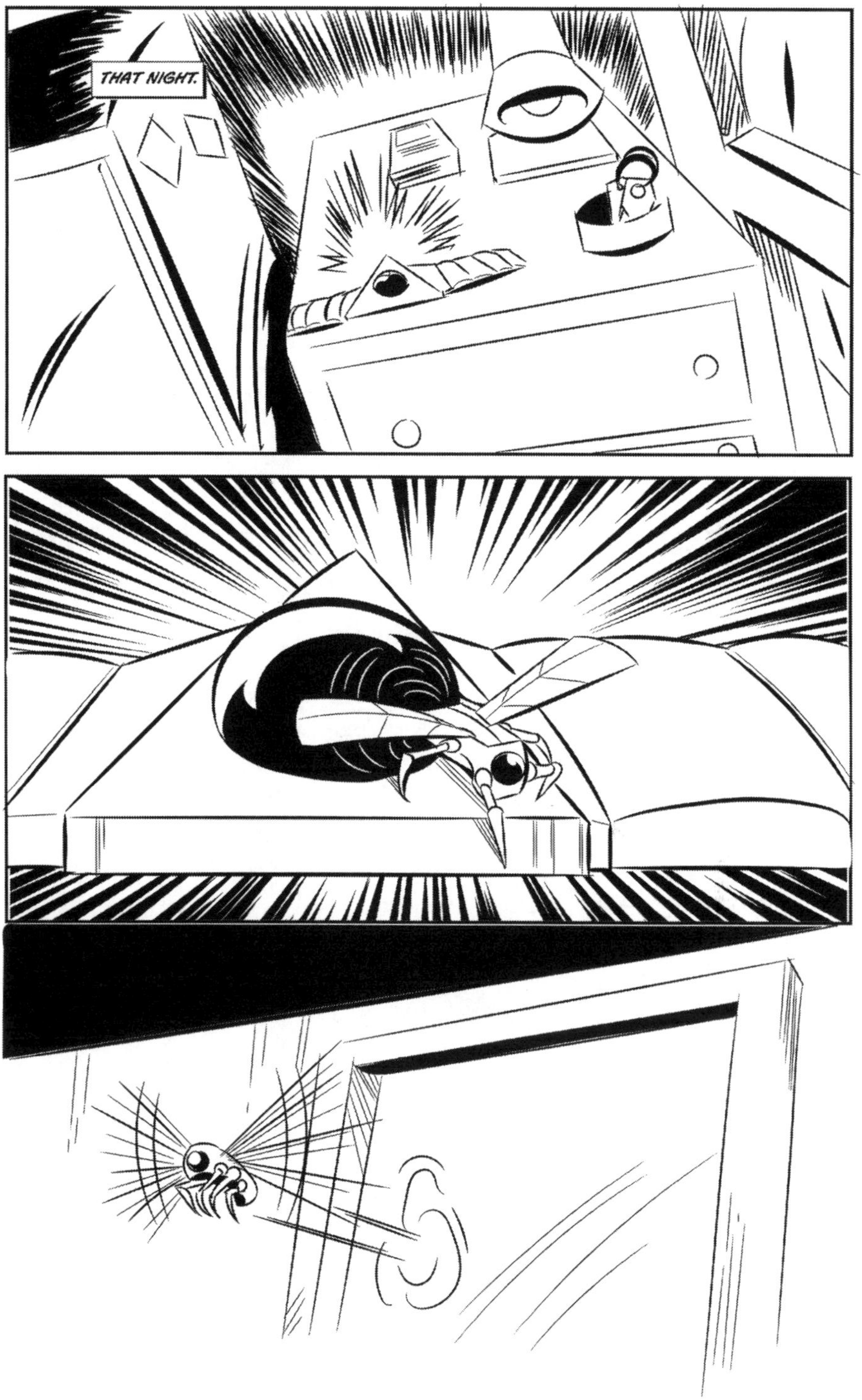

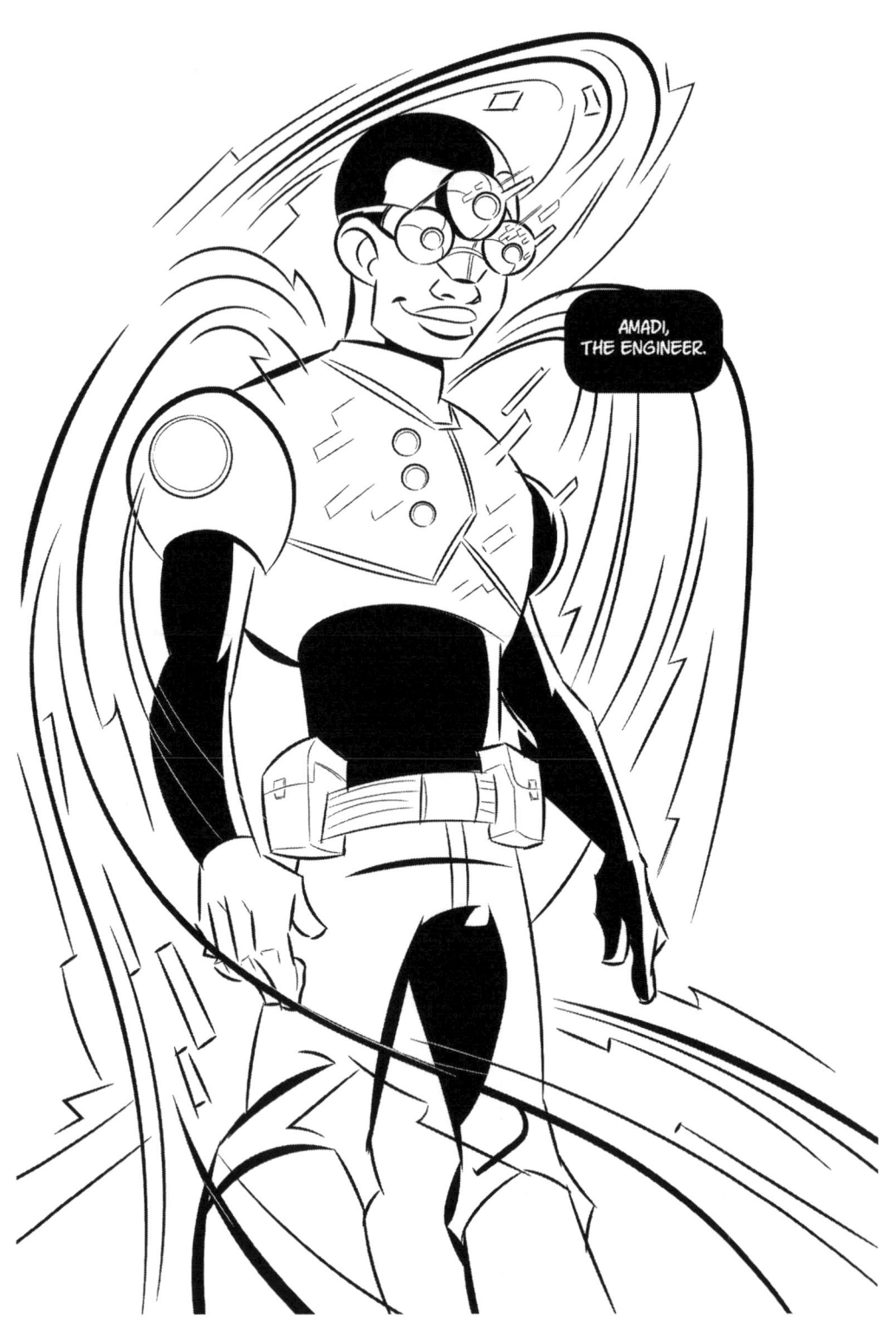

ZAKOW

A GOOD SHOT, CHILD... FOR ALL THE GOOD IT WILL DO YOU...

EH?!?

BRUH WE JUST GETTING STARTED! I'M READY FOR ROUND 2 WHENEVER YOU ARE!

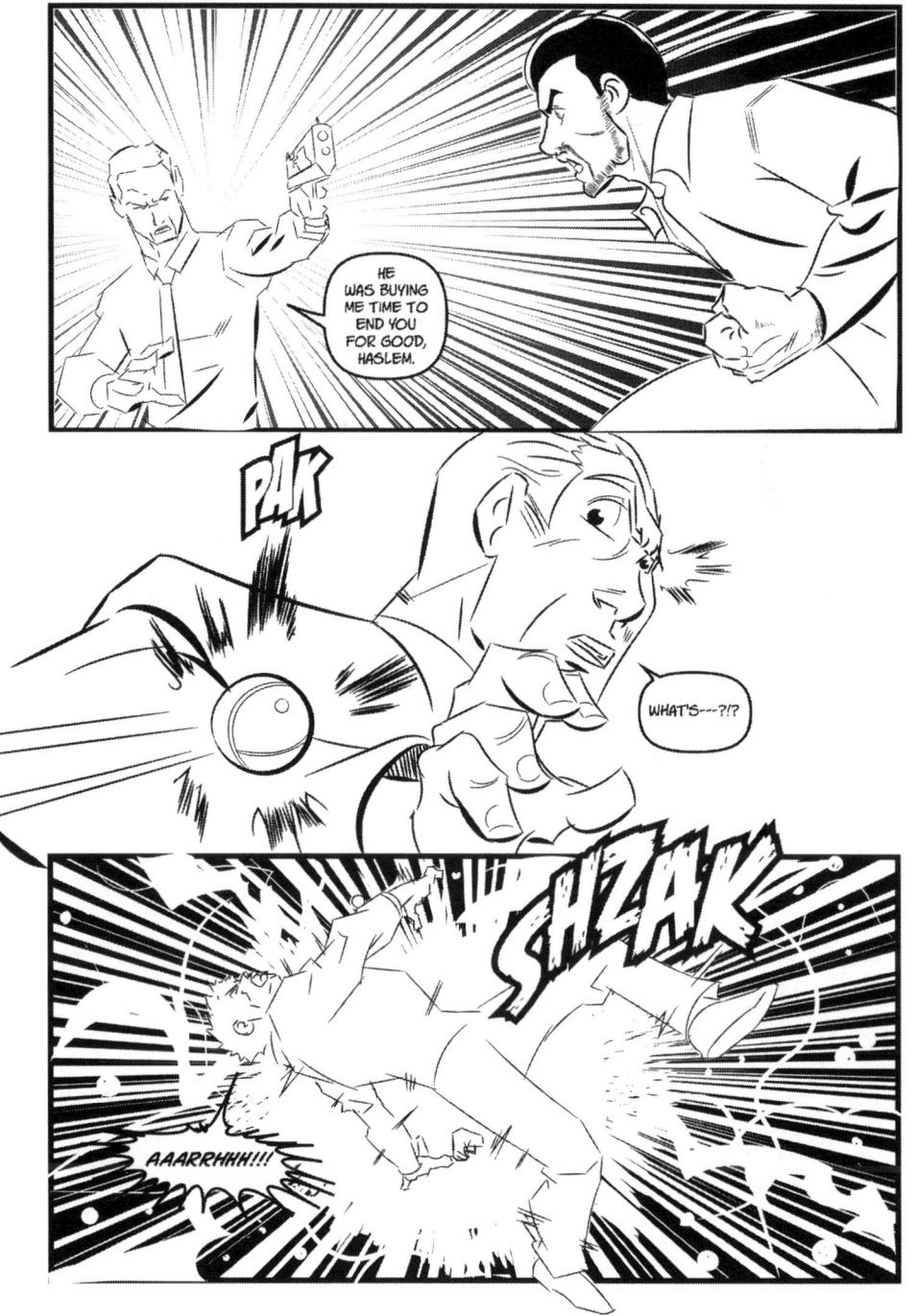

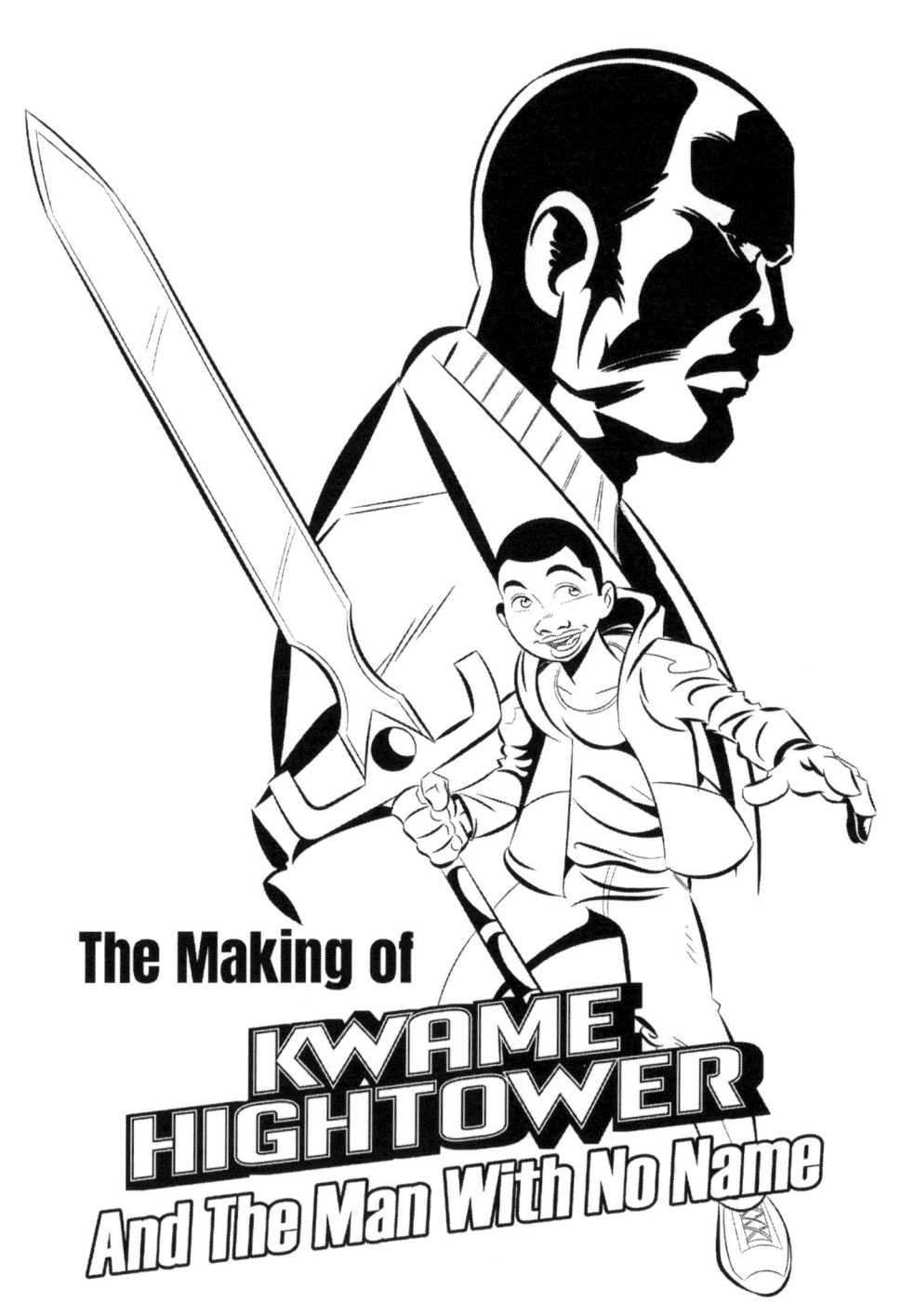

Original David Haslem character designs

I WAS WATCHING A LOT OF LUTHER AT THE TIME I DESIGNED HIM...SO YEAH...IDRIS ELBA INFLUENCE ALL OVER....LOL

Moridan and Gideon studies

SIR PATRICK STEWART WAS MY IINSPIRATION FOR GIDEON'S LOOK AND A COMBO OF BRAD PITT AND LEONARDO DICAPRIO INSPIRED GIDEON

KWAME PIN-UP BY THE INCREDIBLE POW RODRIX!!!

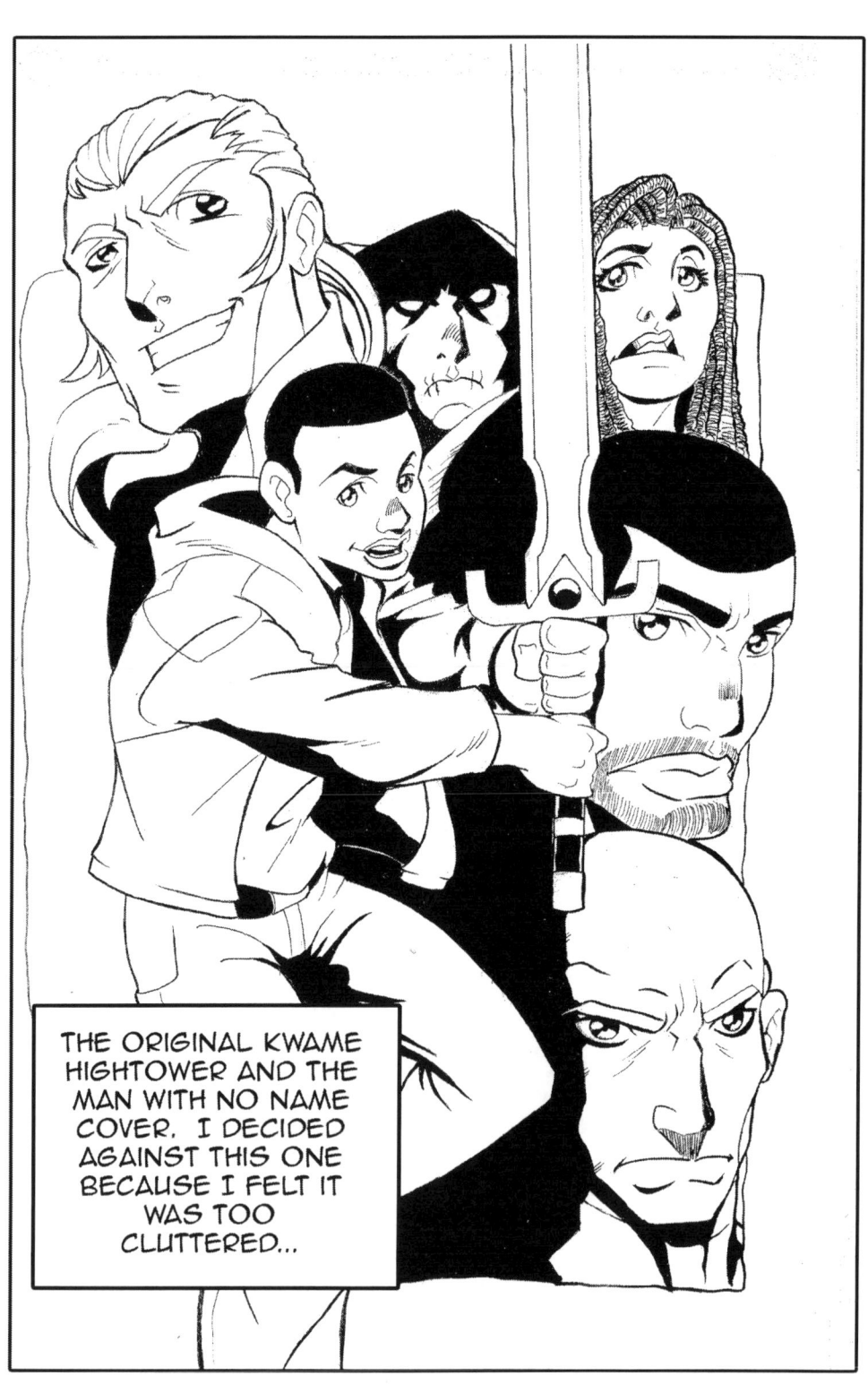

I DECIDED TO REMOVE THESE PAGES WHEN I GOT THE IDEA FOR AN OPENING THAT BETTER HIGHLIGHTED THE DYNAMICS BETWEEN THE THREE ROMAN BROTHERS.

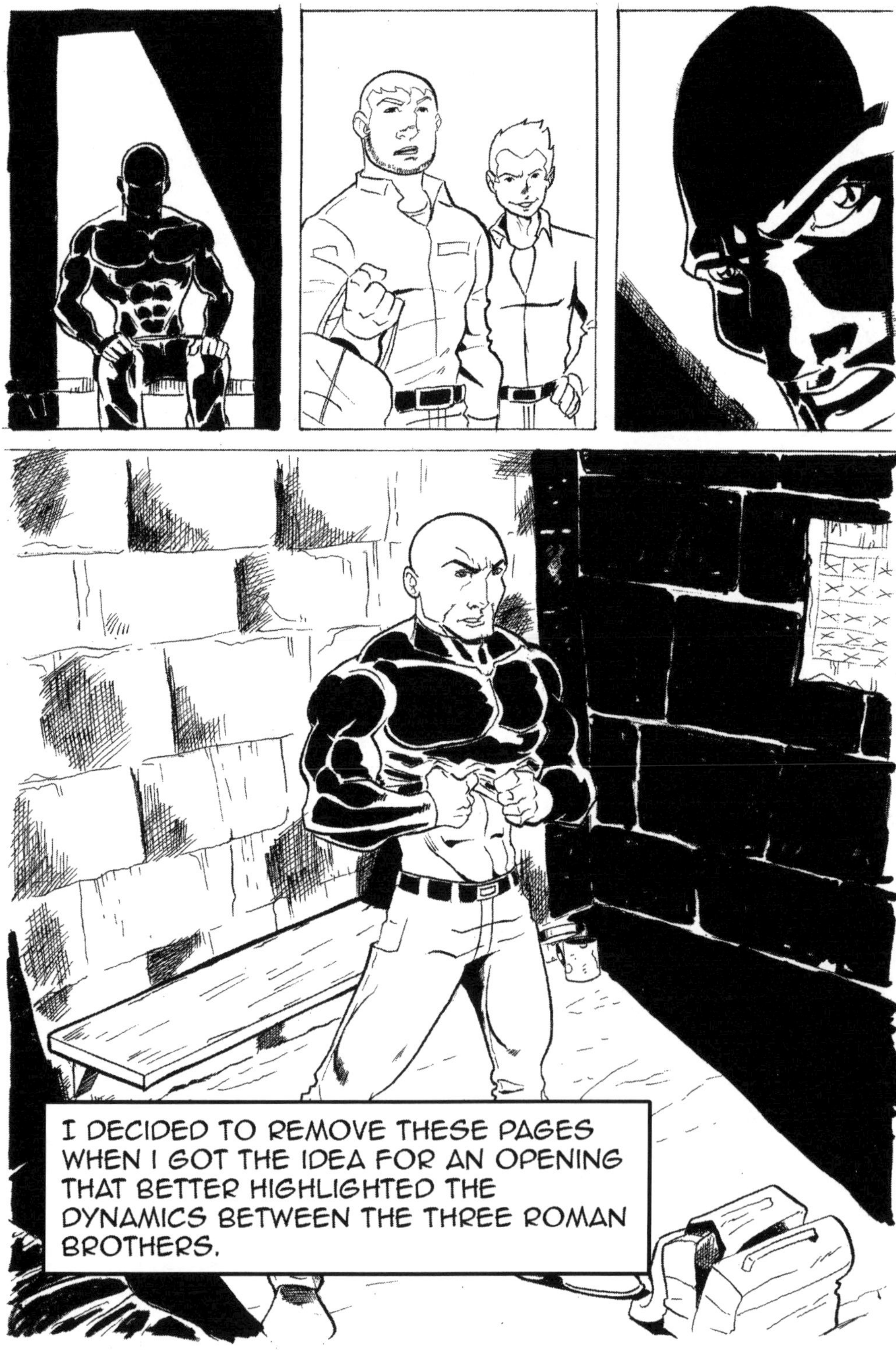

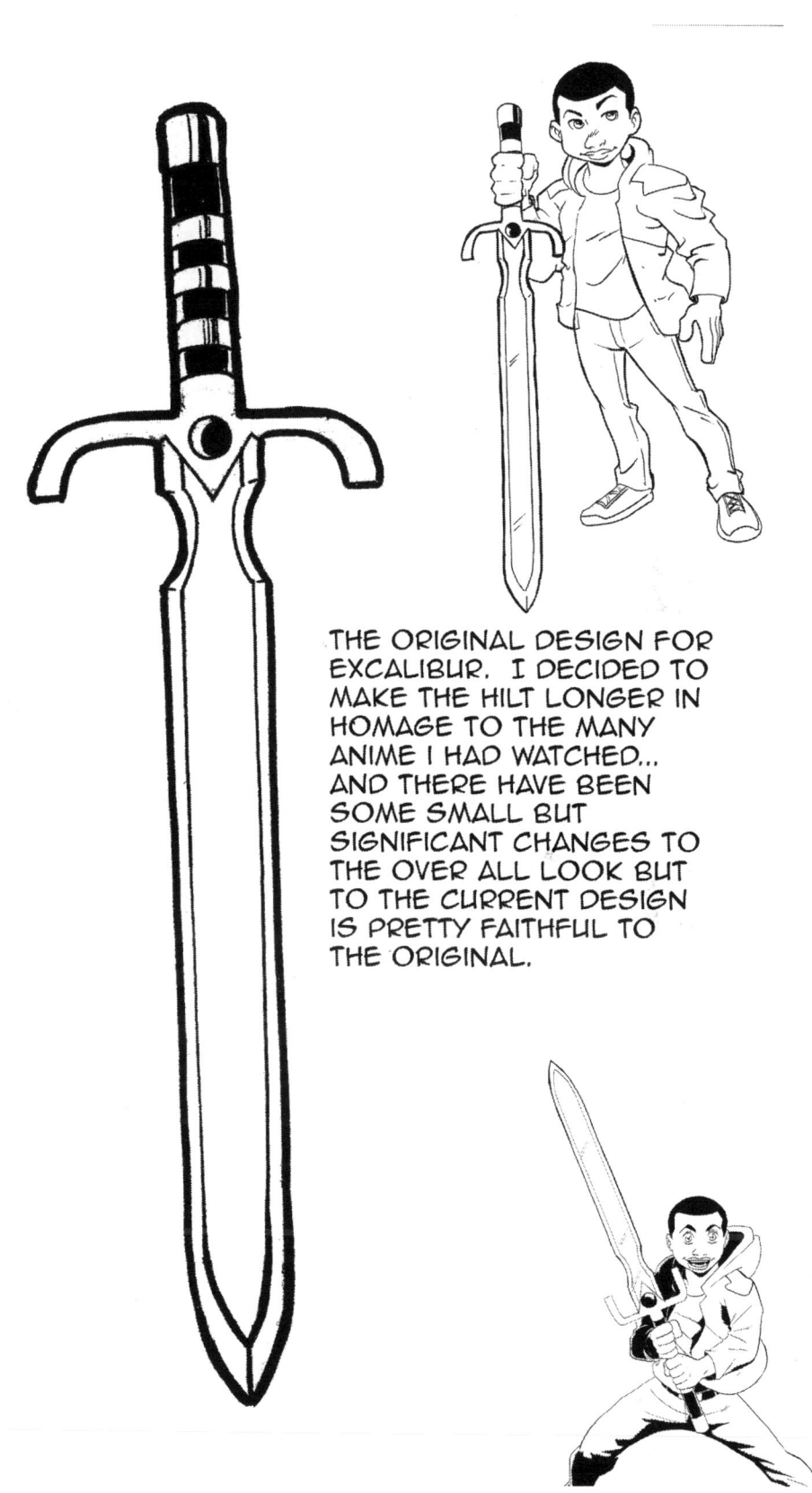

THE ORIGINAL DESIGN FOR EXCALIBUR. I DECIDED TO MAKE THE HILT LONGER IN HOMAGE TO THE MANY ANIME I HAD WATCHED... AND THERE HAVE BEEN SOME SMALL BUT SIGNIFICANT CHANGES TO THE OVER ALL LOOK BUT TO THE CURRENT DESIGN IS PRETTY FAITHFUL TO THE ORIGINAL.

FROM THE AUTHOR

It all started out because I wanted to come up with a property that had elements of Pokémon and Naruto. I wanted it to be a competition-based concept and I wanted it to have a diverse cast with a black lead. I immediately had a name for the kid Kwame Hightower and a cast but not a really solid story. I spent the next couple of years trying to make the concept work and it just didn't; square peg, round hole. Then when I was living in Atlanta while still trying to make the competition aspect work I conceived a potential story line where Kwame became the king of England by accidently pulling Excalibur from the sacred stone. I remember chuckling to myself at the comedy this silly, short concept could generate. Later that year I'd completely dropped Kwame and was onto other things in life.

One day in 2012 I picked the idea back up again, but it wasn't the original concept that intrigued me. It was that little side story I conceived a couple years back. That was the hook! That was the real story! I began working on the concept and wrote the original outline in 2013. Unfortunately, it would take me till late 2016 to bang out a workable script (the concepts kept growing in scale and I had to unpack it all). Then shortly after the election I began working on the art for the book and documenting on my YouTube channel. I would lock in for the entire year of 2017 banging out page after page of art and documenting the journey on my various social media outlets. Hey IG and Twitter fans! What up Facebook fans!

Well now we've finally got to the finish line. Here it is. Kwame Hightower! A true labor of love. My ode to the action and adventure movies and comics that influenced me over the years. Enjoy.

This book is dedicated to my father Robert Gorden (RIP), and my mother Diana Gorden.

I only have one thing to say:
Thank You. For everything.

Made in the USA
Columbia, SC
30 June 2022